Author: Kris Benny
Design by: Kre8ive Design

Hue: "This cool, sunny morning is a welcome delight!
Green lawns and flowers – yellow, blue and white"

Hue: "Every garden is buzzing with life and love
With bugs below and birds above"

"Whose story will unfold on this fine day?
Whose songs will steal our hearts away?"

Hue: "Oh from where do we hear this rhythm holey?
It's none other than our jolly Ollie!

The holes in these leaves are a way to know
That he's a hungry fella from head to toe"

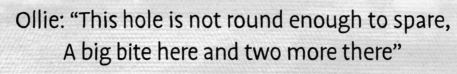
Ollie: "This hole is not round enough to spare,
A big bite here and two more there"

Through those gaps he caught a stunning view
A yellow rose wearing morning dew.

Ollie: "None prettier have I ever seen
In all of my five-week life, I mean"

With a friendly heart he wiggled ahead,
But the thorny guards stopped him and said,

Thorn: "Where do you think you're going now?
Not one step further can we allow!"

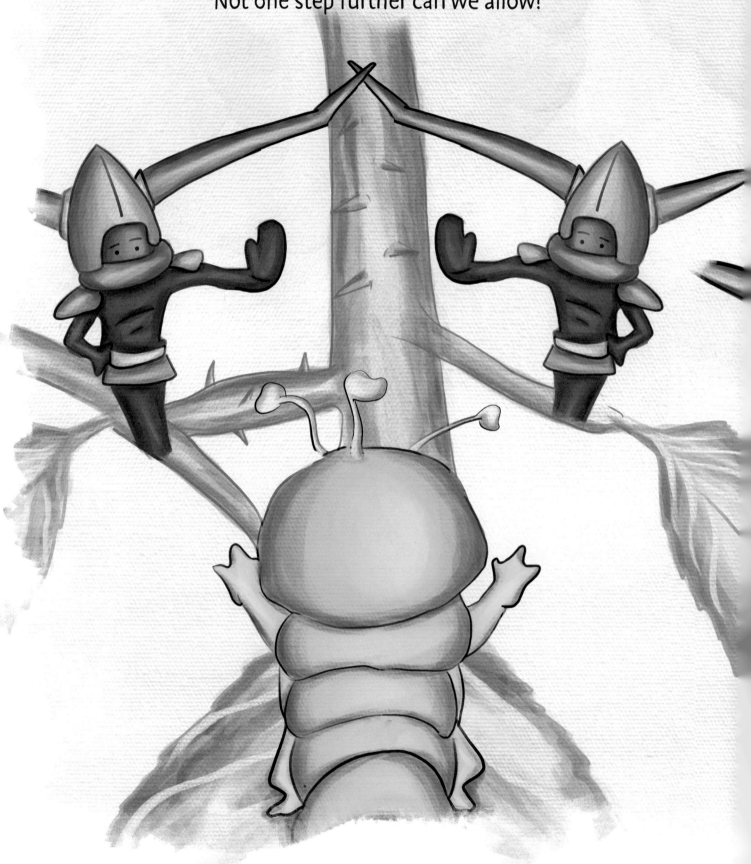

Thorn: "To guard the queen we are the knight
You are better off staying out of our sight"

Saying thus they pushed Ollie away
Making it his life's gloomiest day

But he pulled himself together quickly
He's not afraid of those bullies prickly

Ollie: "I'll build an army strong and true
My friends can come to my rescue"

All the buzzing got his attention now
As a busy bee was taking off above

Ollie: "Hello my friend, dear Billy bee,
will you be the one to help me?"

Ollie revealed what caused him grief
Those thorns were rude beyond belief

The one he admired and wished to greet
Was sadly the one he couldn't meet!

Ollie: "Those thorns could use a lesson or two
Will you be a part of my battle crew?"

Hearing his story Billy bee replied
Sadly that he can't be by his side

Billy: "Today our queen has summoned us all
There is not a way to ignore her call

It pains me to say I can't have your back
But perhaps you can ask our li'l friend Jack?"

Jack and an army of his obedient friends
walked in a line that seemingly never ends

Ollie revealed what caused him grief
Those thorns were rude beyond belief

The one he admired and wished to greet
was sadly the one he couldn't meet

Ollie: "Those thorns could use a lesson or two
Will you be a part of my battle crew?"

Hearing his story Jack quickly replied
And listed why he can't be by his side

Jack: "Winter is close leaving no time for ourselves
we need all hands on stocking our shelves

If you could push it to be in the months cold
Then you have the word of Jack-the-bold"

Ollie: "There's no chance of waiting till after the fall
I must teach those thorns a lesson after all"

Jack: "If your need is urgent and help must come faster
Then there's none better than my cousin, Casper"

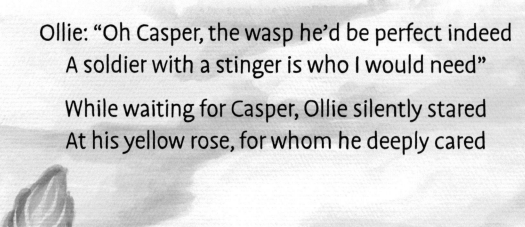

Ollie: "Oh Casper, the wasp he'd be perfect indeed
A soldier with a stinger is who I would need"

While waiting for Casper, Ollie silently stared
At his yellow rose, for whom he deeply cared

Casper: "Hello dear friend, Jack sent me here
For a friend in need I am always near"

Ollie: "There you are! Your help is precious!
To fight those thorn so mean and vicious"

"With a stinger like yours, you'll be a threat
We'll have an advantage, our victory is set!"

Casper: "Whoa, dear Ollie, I'm sorry to disappoint
Boy wasps like me have no stingers to point"

"If only, a girl wasp I had known
She'd be the best in the battle zone"

Ollie thanked Casper and then thought
Stingers or not, this war should be fought

Ollie: "Is there not a friend that I could count on
Is the era of true friendship lost and gone?"

If a friend with wings could give him a ride
Or even from high up he quietly spied

He can learn their ways and win with ease
Reaching his rose would then be a breeze

And for that he knew just the right one
With whose help his job is nearly done.

He heard Louie singing in rhythm and rhyme
Playing a fiddle, having a jolly good time

As he approached his musical friend
He hoped that all his troubles would end

Ollie wiggled to Louie with a righteous purpose
If he'd agree or not, made him utterly nervous

Boldly he revealed what caused him grief
Those thorns were rude beyond belief

The one he admired and wished to greet
Was sadly the one he couldn't meet

Ollie: "Those thorns should learn a lesson or two
Will you be a part of my battle crew?"

Louie carefully heard every single bit
He silently wondered at Ollie's grit

Louie: "So the thorns were doing their job as knights
Protecting their queen from bugs and bites"

"And you adore the rose with all your heart
But to reach her those thorn you must outsmart"

"Oh, you too my jolly dear friend, Ollie
Turn out to commit the very same folly

In an urge to fulfill all we ever ask for
Should we always resort to a mindless war?

Love or peace has never been gained
By the fighting swords of an army trained"

"In a little poem write all you feel
And sing to her your heart's appeal

In a tune that only you could play
Go simply steal her heart away

Or perhaps forget all worries and cling
To the joy that comes from rhythm and sing"

Ollie got a large dose of wisdom drink
He needed a place to curl up and think

He reached a branch far away from the ground
And gave in to the urge to weave all around

A sturdy silken soundless room
To let him enjoy his boundless gloom

Two weeks passed in deepest thought
To know that wars should never be fought

He began to respect those thorny knight
They protect their queen with all their might

And if sometimes friends can't lend a hand
They have a good reason, you must understand

To shut one's mind to another's perspective
Prevents one from being fair and objective

Ollie: "Oh no! My home has started to crack
The list of troubles I can no longer track"

"The one I admire and wish to greet
Is still the one I cannot meet"

"Wait... I feel a strange ticklish twitch
Will a wiggle fix this ill-timed itch?"

"Upon my back there's something queer
Umm... what is this colorful velvet here?"

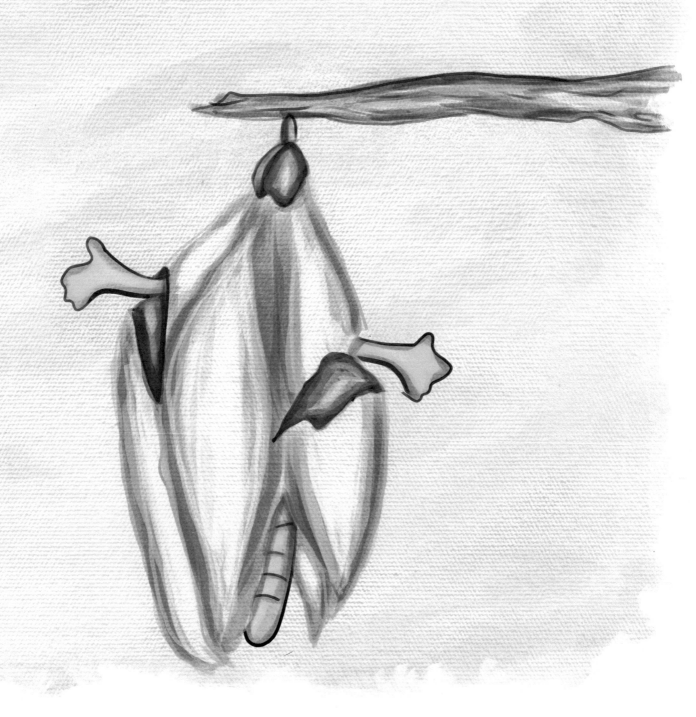

"Oh my, oh my, this cannot be
Perhaps a dream is what I see"

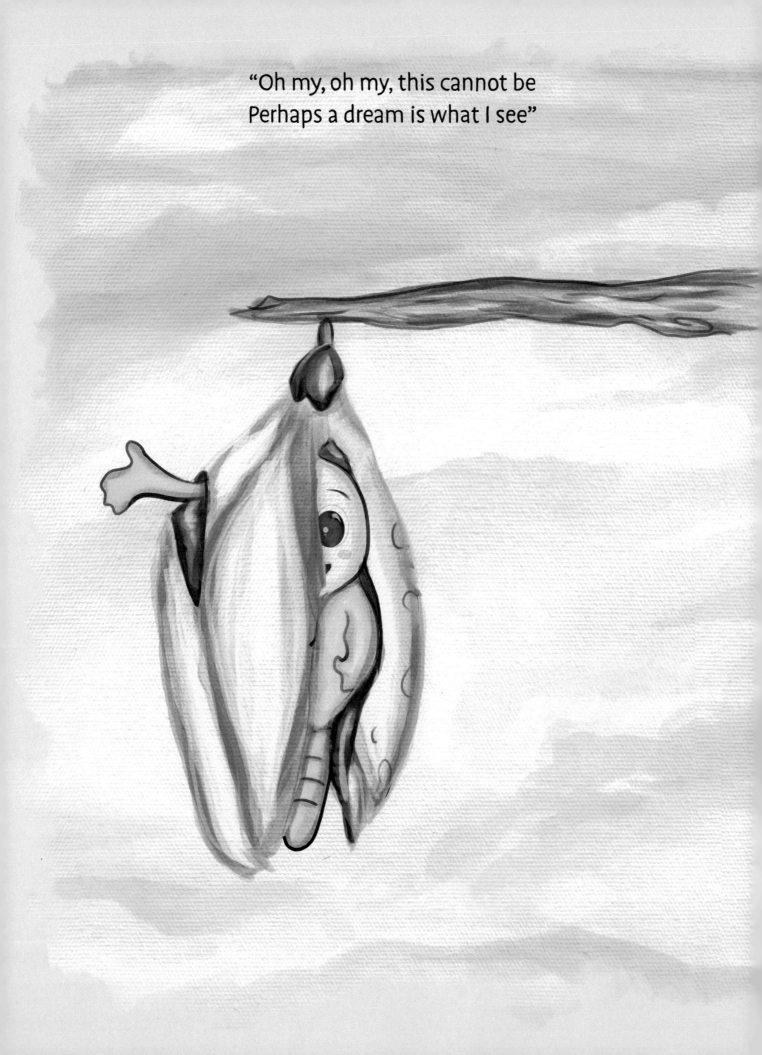

"How is it that I grew a wing?
Will I soon hear angels sing?"

"To heaven, though, I shall be late
I'll meet my rose and explain my fate"

Hue: "Hey Ollie you're now a butterfly
Use those wings and soar up high

Show the world your vibrant wings
Tell us what joy this change brings"

Ollie: "This is no less than a dream come true
Who could I thank for this life so new?

Thank you, Hue, for letting me know
I'm sure you know where I wish to go"

Ollie: "Oh dear, she's even prettier up close
Hello my queen, my love, my rose!

Could this even be true what I now see?
Such love in her eyes, and it's all for me!"

Hue: "What a joy to see such a happy ending
Best wishes their way, let's keep on sending"

The End

Did you know?

The life of a butterfly is fascinating!

There are four stages: An Egg, Larva also known as caterpillar, Pupa also known as chrysalis and then a Butterfly!

2 Caterpillar
2 - 5 weeks

1 Eggs
3 - 7 days

Metamorphosis

There are many species of butterflies and each one has different duration for each of these stages. But typically the egg stage lasts 3 - 7 days, caterpillar stage lasts 2 - 5 weeks, pupa stage for 1 - 3 weeks and then emerges a beautiful butterfly.

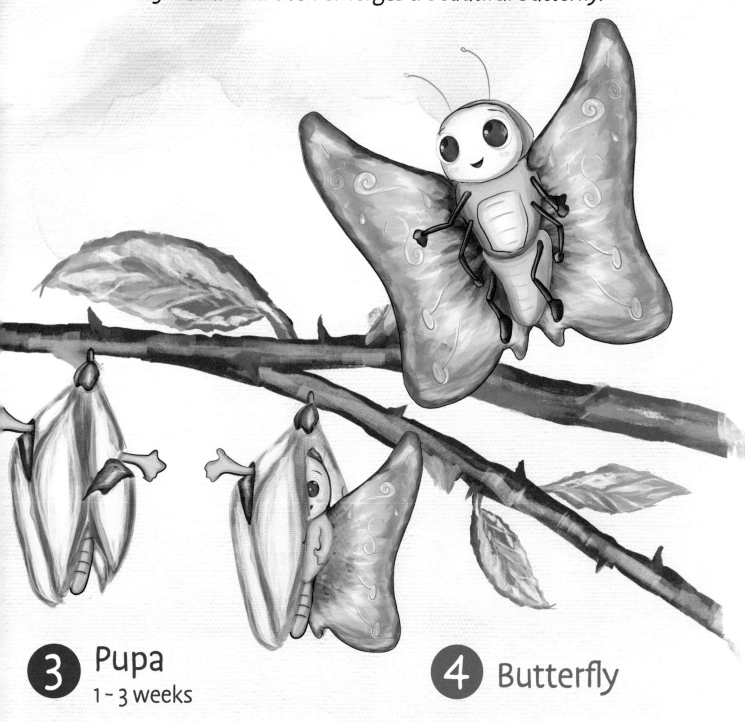

3 Pupa
1 - 3 weeks

4 Butterfly